The Mystery of the Haunted Scarecrow

by Fran Manushkin
illustrated by Tammie Lyon

PICTURE WINDOW BOOKS
a capstone imprint

Published by Picture Window Books, an imprint of Capstone
1710 Roe Crest Drive, North Mankato, Minnesota 56003
capstonepub.com

Library of Congress Cataloging-in-Publication Data
Names: Manushkin, Fran, author. | Lyon, Tammie, illustrator.
Title: The mystery of the haunted scarecrow / by Fran Manushkin ; illustrated by Tammie Lyon.
Description: North Mankato : Picture Window Books, an imprint of Capstone, 2022. | Series: Katie Woo and Pedro mysteries | Audience: Ages 5-7. | Audience: Grades K-1. | Summary: A frowning scarecrow at Aunt Carmen's farm frightens Katie until Pedro reveals that it is not haunted.
Identifiers: LCCN 2021055398 (print) | LCCN 2021055399 (ebook) | ISBN 9781666335798 (hardcover) | ISBN 9781666335743 (paperback) | ISBN 9781666335750 (ebook PDF)
Subjects: LCSH: Woo, Katie (Fictitious character)—Juvenile fiction. | Chinese Americans—Juvenile fiction. | Hispanic Americans—Juvenile fiction. | Scarecrows—Juvenile fiction. | Detective and mystery stories. | CYAC: Mystery and detective stories. | Chinese Americans—Fiction. | Hispanic Americans—Fiction. | Scarecrows—Fiction. | LCGFT: Detective and mystery fiction.
Classification: LCC PZ7.M3195 Mw 2022 (print) | LCC PZ7.M3195 (ebook) | DDC 813.54 [E]—dc23/eng/20211215
LC record available at https://lccn.loc.gov/2021055398
LC ebook record available at https://lccn.loc.gov/2021055399

Design Elements by Shutterstock: Darcraft, Magnia
Designed by Dina Her

Printed and bound in the USA. PO4882

Table of Contents

Chapter 1

On the Farm

Pedro was with Katie at his Aunt Carmen's farm. There was so much to see and to do!

Aunt Carmen grew corn—lots and lots of corn!

"Crows like eating my corn," said Aunt Carmen. "So I got a scarecrow."

The scarecrow had long arms made of cornstalks. He had long legs stuffed with straw.

“The scarecrow is wearing Aunt Carmen’s old jeans,” said Pedro.

“And her sun hat,” said Katie.

"Why is the scarecrow frowning?" asked Katie. "He looks spooky!"

"Yes!" said Pedro. "He makes me shiver."

Crows came flying by.
Caw! Caw! CAW! They
wanted to eat the corn.
But the scarecrow scared
them away.

Chapter 2

Spooky Scarecrow

"Let's pick some corn for lunch," said Pedro.

"Yum!" Katie smiled. "I love corn with lots of butter."

Katie began picking. The cornstalks were tall, and the scarecrow was spooky.

His black-button eyes stared at Katie.

"I wish you would smile," said Katie. "I'm getting spooked!"

“Yikes!” Katie yelled. “Something is creeping up my leg!”

Was it a bug?

Or a worm?

Or a long snake?

No! It was Pedro tickling Katie with a corn tassel.

"I got you!" he yelled.

Katie giggled. "You are silly."

Chapter 3

Is It Haunted?

Katie asked the scarecrow, "Isn't Pedro silly?"

Pedro told Katie, "You are the silly one. That scarecrow cannot talk."

“Uh-oh!” said Katie.

“Something big and dark is following us. We better run!”

Pedro didn’t run. Pedro laughed. “Katie, that’s the scarecrow’s shadow,” he said.

Katie shook her finger at the scarecrow. "Stop trying to scare me."

"*Whooooo?*" said the scarecrow. "*Whooo? Whooo? WHOOOOOOOOOOOOOOO?*"

“He’s talking!” yelled Katie. “I’m running! I told you he’s spooky!”

“Stop!” said Pedro. “Come and look closer.”

Katie looked closely at the scarecrow's hat. "I see a nest!" said Katie.

"Yes," said Pedro. "With two owlets and their mom."

"You are not haunted!" Katie smiled. "You are a home for a family."

Katie changed the scarecrow's frown into a smile. A big, big smile!

And they hooted all the way home.

About the Author

Fran Manushkin is the author of Katie Woo, the highly acclaimed fan-favorite early-reader series, as well as the popular Pedro series. Her other books include *Happy in Our Skin*, *Plenty of Hugs!*, *Baby, Come Out!*, and the best-selling board books *Big Girl Panties* and *Big Boy Underpants*. There is a real Katie Woo: Fran's great-niece, but she doesn't get into as much trouble as the Katie in the books. Fran lives in New York City, three blocks from Central Park, where she can often be found bird-watching and daydreaming. She writes at her dining room table, without the help of her naughty cats, Goldy and Chaim.

About the Illustrator

Tammie Lyon, the illustrator of the Katie Woo and Pedro series, says that these characters are two of her favorites. Tammie has illustrated work for Disney, Scholastic, Simon and Schuster, Penguin, HarperCollins, and Amazon Publishing, to name a few. She is also an author/illustrator of her own stories. Her first picture book, *Olive and Snowflake*, was released to starred reviews from *Kirkus* and *School Library Journal*. Tammie lives in Cincinnati, Ohio, with her husband, Lee, and two dogs, Amos and Artie. She spends her days working in her home studio in the woods, surrounded by wildlife and, of course, two mostly-always-sleeping dogs.

Glossary

cornstalk (KORN-stawk)—the stem of a corn plant

haunted (HAWN-tid)—to have ghosts

owlet (OU-lit)—a baby owl

shiver (SHIV-er)—to shake slightly with fear

spooky (SPOO-kee)—scary or creepy

tickle (TIK-uhl)—to touch lightly to make a tingly or itchy feeling

All About Mysteries

A mystery is a story where the main characters must figure out a puzzle or solve a crime. Let's think about *The Mystery of the Haunted Scarecrow.*

Plot

In a mystery, the plot focuses on solving a problem. What is the problem in this story?

Clues

To solve a mystery, readers should look for clues. What are some of the clues in this mystery?

Red Herrings

Red herrings are bad clues. They do not help solve the mystery. Sometimes they even make the mystery harder to solve. What clues in this story were red herrings?

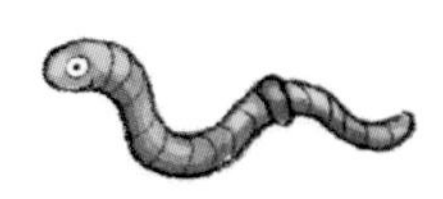

Thinking About the Story

1. List the reasons Katie thought the scarecrow was haunted. Next to each reason, write the explanation for what it really was.
2. Katie and Pedro got spooked by the scarecrow. Have you ever gotten spooked? Explain how it felt.
3. Imagine that Pedro and Katie told Aunt Carmen they thought the scarecrow was haunted. What do you think Aunt Carmen would have said or done?
4. Pretend you are Katie or Pedro and write Aunt Carmen a thank you note for your time on her farm. Be sure to tell her your favorite part of your visit.

Spooky or Sweet? You Choose!

The scarecrow in this story was spooky until Katie gave it a sweet smile. You can make your own scarecrow with this project. Best of all, you can decide if you want a spooky or sweet scarecrow, all by what type of face you give it!

Make a Paper Bag Scarecrow

What you need:

- cardstock in a variety of colors
- scissors
- markers
- small brown paper bag
- raffia or yarn
- glue
- old newspapers

What you do:

1. Using the cardstock, make a hat for your scarecrow. Make sure it is a little wider than the top of the paper bag. Try a straw sun hat or witch's hat. Add details to your hat with markers or pieces of card stock.

2. Draw a scarecrow face on one side of your paper bag. A smiley face will make it sweet. An angry face will make it spooky.

3. Cut pieces of the raffia or yarn, about 14 inches long. Fold the pieces in half and glue them near the top of the bag. This is your scarecrow's hair.

4. Glue the hat over the top of the bag. The hat should cover the top of the raffia or yarn.

5. Stuff the bag with crumpled old newspapers and glue it shut. Place it on display to give your friends and family smiles or shivers!

Solve more mysteries with Katie and Pedro!

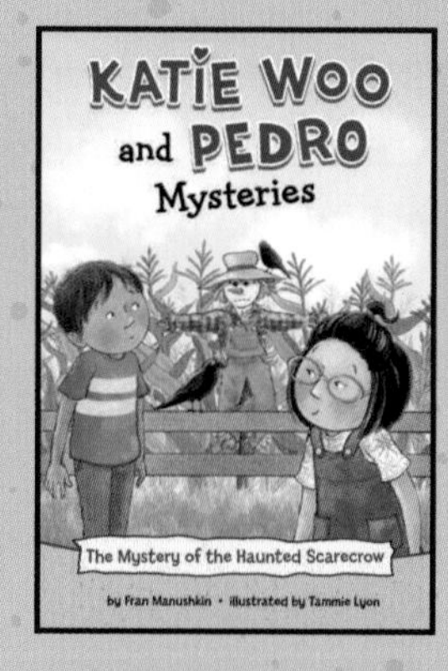

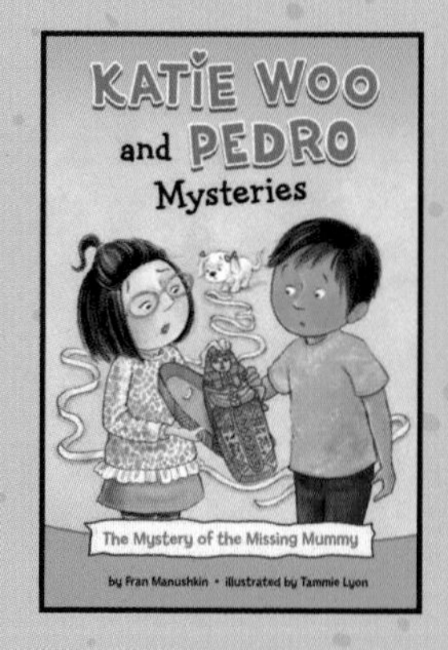

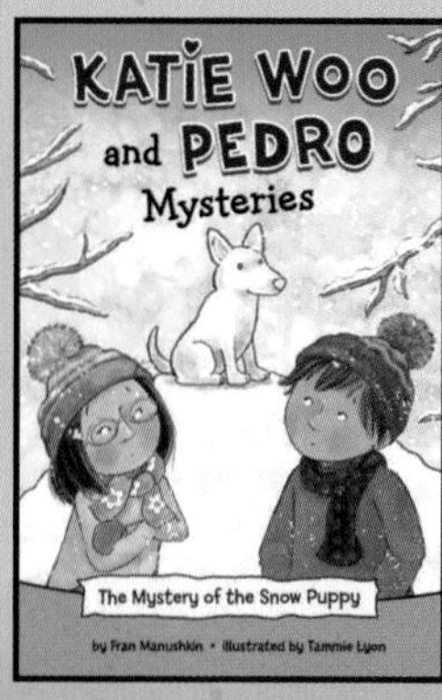

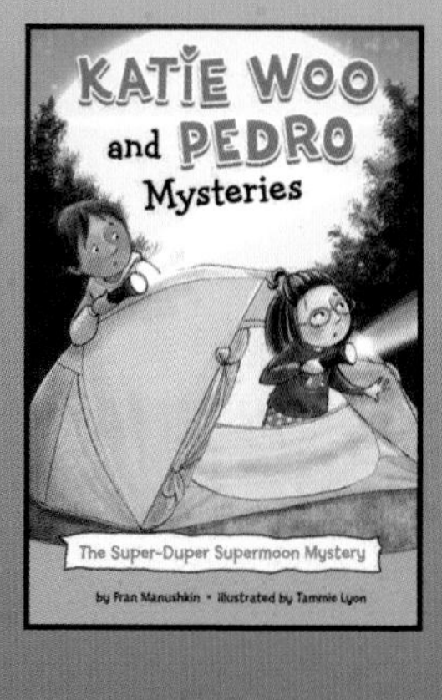